FRANKLIN PARK PUBLIC LIBRARY

FRANKLIN PARK, ILL.

Each borrower is held responsible for all library material drawn on his card and for fines accruing on the same. No material will be issued until such fine has been paid.

All injuries to library material beyond reasonable wear and all losses shall be made good to the satisfaction of the Librarian.

Replacement costs will be billed after 42 days overdue.

Merry Christmas, Princess Dinosaur!
By Jill Kastner

GREENWILLOW BOOKS An Imprint of HarperCollinsPublishers

For Greta,
who wants to be a
dinosaur veterinarian
when she grows up

Merry Christmas, Princess Dinosaur!
Copyright © 2002 by Jill Kastner
All rights reserved.
Printed in Singapore by Tien Wah Press.
www.harperchildrens.com

Watercolors and pen and ink were used for the full-color art.
The text type is Futura Heavy.

Library of Congress Cataloging-in-Publication Data
Kastner, Jill.
Merry Christmas, Princess Dinosaur! / by Jill Kastner.
    p.   cm.
"Greenwillow Books."
Summary: On Christmas Eve, Princess Dinosaur exchanges presents
with her friends and tries to stay awake to see Santa Claus.
ISBN 0-06-000471-1 (trade). ISBN 0-06-000472-X (lib. bdg.)
[1. Christmas—Fiction. 2. Toys—Fiction. 3. Dinosaurs—Fiction.]
I. Title. PZ7.K1563 Me 2002   [E]—dc21   2001054789

1 2 3 4 5 6 7 8 9 10 First Edition

Christmas is here!
It's Princess Dinosaur's favorite time of year.
She has presents for all her friends.
"But Christmas isn't until tomorrow,"
says Bettina Esmerelda Louise.
"Shouldn't we wait?" asks Turtle.

Princess Dinosaur is
too excited to wait.
She wants her friends
to open their presents
right away.
So they do.

Bettina Esmerelda Louise gets
a new necklace. There is a
fun rock for Cowboy Tex
and his pals to play with.

Then we go for a

boat rid

Princess Dinosaur
gives Piggy, Turtle,
and Teddy a book
that she made herself.

Soon it's time for bed, but
Princess Dinosaur can't sleep.
"Where are you going,
    Princess Dinosaur?" asks Piggy.
"Santa won't come unless
    we're asleep,"
Cowboy Gus says.

But Princess Dinosaur wants to make sure
everything is ready for Santa.
So she heads downstairs.
"WATCH OUT FOR SPOTS!" everyone yells.

Princess Dinosaur
is excited.

Being excited
makes her hungry.

Wait!

There is one more present

Princess Dinosaur
must deliver

before Santa comes.

"Merry Christmas!"
Princess Dinosaur yells.
"I hope you like it!"

And he does!

When will Santa arrive?
How will he know where
Princess Dinosaur lives?
She has an idea.

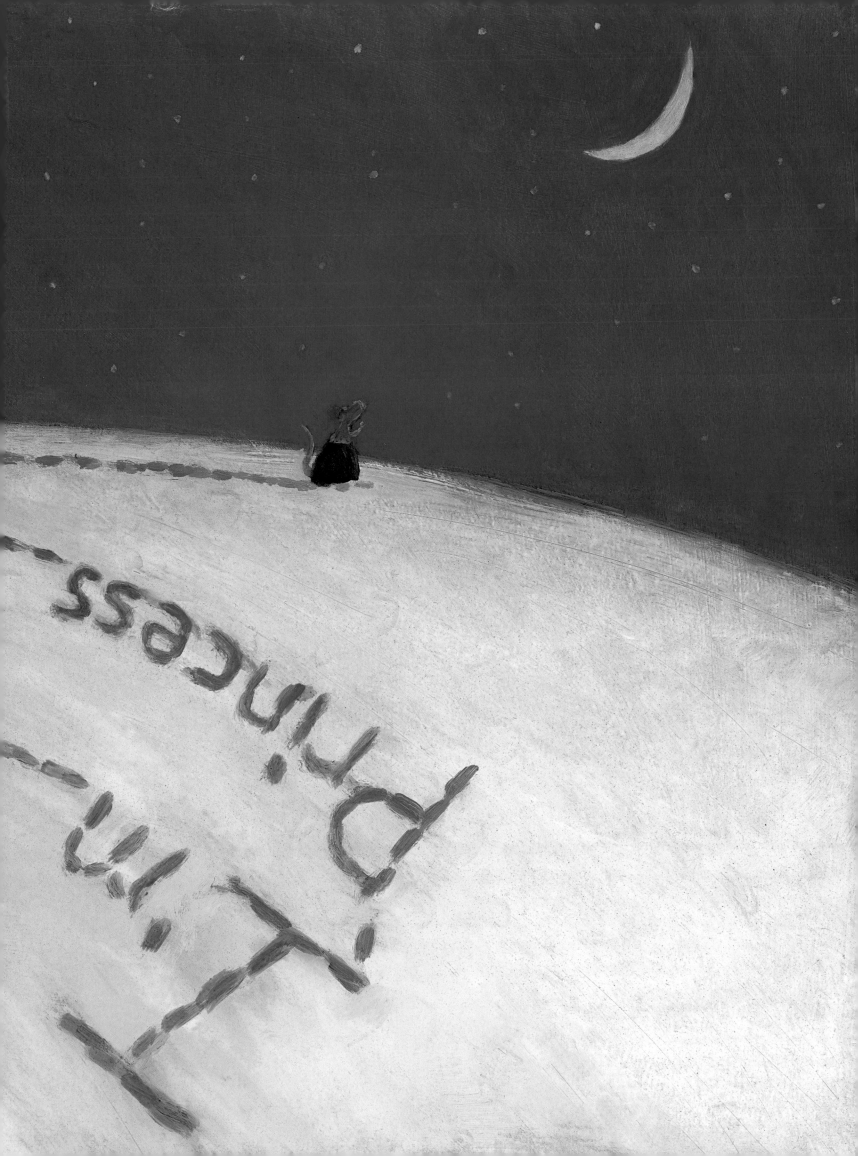

Is the roof too steep
for Santa's reindeer?

Will Santa
be able to fit
down the chimney?

What's that
red light in the sky?
Is it Rudolph?

Hurry!

Santa is coming!

Princess Dinosaur
needs a place to hide.

Quick,
up the tree!

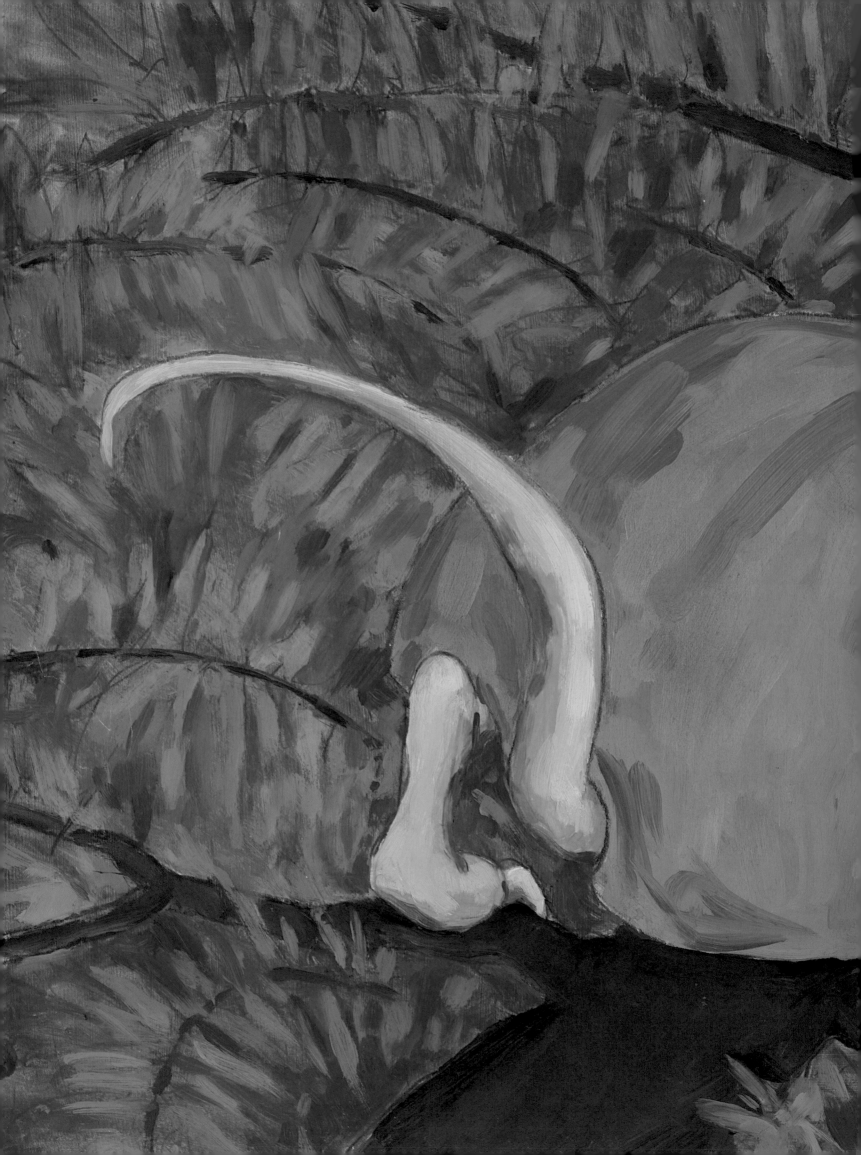

CLIMB,
PRINCESS DINOSAUR,
CLIMB!

Princess Dinosaur

waits . . . and waits . . . and waits.

Where is Santa?

Zzzzzzz . . . . .

Wow!
Look at all those presents!
Santa must have come
while Princess Dinosaur
was asleep.
She can't wait
to tell her friends.

Christmas is here!

For Spots
From Santa

Yippee!

Uh-oh, Spots is awake!

Do something, Princess Dinosaur!

For Spots-
om Santa

Here, Spots.
Catch!

Later, everyone opens
a gift from Santa.
Princess Dinosaur
goes first.

Just what
she's always wanted!

Merry Christmas,
Princess Dinosaur!